The Giant's Boy

Story by Joy Cowley

The giant's boy felt stormy.
He frowned black clouds.

3

He stamped thunder and lightning.

He shouted hail.

He yelled a gale.

He cried rain, rain, rain.

7

"What a storm!" the people said, and they ran into their houses.

8

"Poor boy!" said the giant.
"Let me hug you better."

The wind stopped.

The rain stopped.

"I feel better now,"
said the giant's boy.

The giant's boy stood on his head
and smiled a rainbow.

14

The giant's boy danced blue sky.

The giant's boy laughed and laughed
a sunshine day.